Fatal Revenge

A Gripping Suspense Thriller

Teagan Stone Series
Book 7

Ava S. King

304 Publishing Company

 Created with Vellum

Latest Releases: Ava S. King

Agent Red Fatal Memory Teagan Stone Book 1

Agent Red Fatal Target Teagan Stone Book 2

Agent Red Fatal Crime Teagan Stone Book 3

Agent Red Fatal Justice Teagan Stone Book 4

Agent Red Fatal Enemy Teagan Stone Book 5

Mirror of Lies—Jessica Smith Book 1

Agent Red Fatal Death Teagan Stone Book 6

Mirror of Lust—Jessica Smith Book 2

Agent Red Fatal Revenge Teagan Stone Book 7

Agent Red Fatal Pursuit Teagan Stone Book 8

Upcoming Releases (2023/2024)

Mirror of Danger—Jessica Smith Book 3

Chris Harris Mystery/Thriller Series

Agent Red Fatal Attack Teagan Stone Book 9

Agent Red Fatal Mission Teagan Stone Book 10

I want to dedicate this book to my family and friends.

You are always with me, no matter where I go, and everything you've taught me has made me a better person.

Disclaimer

A work of fiction contains strong language and explicit content and is only intended for mature readers. The story may contain unconventional situations, language, and sexual encounters that may offend some readers. This book is for mature readers (18+).

Introduction

Sign-up for Ava S. King's mailing list for news, new releases, and special offers.

www.authoravasking.com

Synopsis

A fast-paced action-adventure political thriller with unforgettable characters and heart-pounding suspense.

Teagan Stone and her team have dealt with many threats in the past, but this time the danger is hard to identify. When a congressman is murdered, Teagan and her team are called in to investigate. Matters are complicated because the congressman was dating a foreign leader. A nation's peace hangs in the balance, and Teagan and her team are on the clock to find the truth. When they discover they're up against a serial killer, they realize their lives hang in the balance.

Can Teagan identify the killer hellbent on revenge, or will she pay the ultimate price?

Chapter One

Teagan lifted her arms and counted to five before placing the dumbbells back on the weight machine. Releasing slow breaths, she grabbed the towel to wipe the sweat from her face and watched the sunrise through the office gym window. She smiled as she thought of her husband snoring as she'd left early this morning.

"What are you doing here so early?" Daughtrey asked, strolling in with a gym bag on his shoulder.

Teagan shrugged. "Couldn't sleep." She gulped her water and tossed the empty bottle in the trash as she moved to the treadmill.

Daughtrey grinned and dropped his bag on the ground next to the weight machine. "Same."

"I heard you had a date the other night." Teagan switched on the treadmill and set it to the right pace.

Daughtrey chuckled as he leaned over to set the weight limit. "More like a one-night stand."

The team had earned some downtime after their last case, and Teagan wanted everyone to have a break for a few weeks. She'd moved the upcoming cases to other departments and the local police. It felt good not to have a crazed terrorist on the loose or a corrupt politician trying to take them down.

Teagan scoffed at how the guys were into kicking it rather than settling down with someone and starting a family. The guys loved her kids, but none wanted the tie of a spouse they had to check in with when they were on missions.

"One day, you're going to catch something," Teagan joked.

Daughtrey frowned and opened his mouth to reply when Spider marched in.

"We just got a case." Spider's expression was grim.

"Since when?" Daughtrey asked, slamming the weight onto the stand.

Spider slid his hands into his pockets. "The local police want us to take a look at something."

"We never do local cases." Teagan stopped the treadmill.

Spider exhaled heavily. "I already told them, but this isn't your typical murder."

Teagan dropped her head back with a groan. She hated that the team was being disturbed on their time off, but it must be a high-priority case if the president had signed off on it.

Teagan headed for her office with Daughtrey and Spider. A green light illuminated, and the door opened as she applied her hand to the security scan. Grabbing the remote, she turned on the TV and sank into her chair behind her desk. A case file sat on the surface, and she opened it, glancing over the contents. The sun wasn't fully up, and a headache was already creeping in around her temples. It was going to be a long day.

"What do you have so far?" she asked Spider.

Spider leaned over the desk and tapped his fingers on the pictures in the file. "Looks like an open and shut case of robbery."

"Anything valuable taken?" Teagan asked, grimacing at the pictures of a woman with a bullet hole in her head.

Daughtrey flung his hands out. "We're on a break. Why can't they handle it themselves?"

Spider looked between Teagan and Daughtrey. "The police commissioner spoke with the president and wants us to consult."

As soon as he said the words, her office line rang, followed by her cell.

"What are the odds?" Teagan shook her head. She grabbed her purse from behind her desk and plucked out her cell as Spider answered the office line.

Teagan pinned her eyes on the TV screen. "Mr. President. Good morning."

"Director Stone. Glad you're still answering my calls," President Sanders joked.

Teagan slumped in her chair as news of another murder at a local bar near downtown Times Square scrolled along the bottom of the screen. "President Sanders, of course we always answer."

President Sanders sighed. "You may not feel the same way after this call."

Teagan sat forward in her chair again as Spider and Daughtrey settled in the chairs in front of her desk. "Let me be the judge."

"The commissioner is involved and wants the best.

You know my stand on cracking down on crime," President Sanders said.

Teagan clenched the phone. "You've already got my vote, Sir. Leave out the fluff."

President Sanders chuckled. "That's why I like you, Teagan. Direct and to the point."

Teagan put the call on speaker and placed it on the desk. "I have you on speaker phone with Spider and Daughtrey, Mr. President."

"Gentleman," President Sanders greeted.

"Mr. President," Spider and Daughtrey said in unison.

"When the commissioner initially called, I told him we couldn't help, but we have too many bodies turning up with the same MO," President Sanders explained.

Teagan glanced at the pictures in the file. "Spider brought me one folder. How many more are there?"

President Sanders sighed down the line. "Unfortunately, we have a serial killer on the loose."

"Serial killer?" Teagan whispered.

"*Breaking News. We have reports that the French Minister of Arms, Penny Fernsby, has just landed in New York,*" Channel Seven reported in the background.

"What makes you think this is a serial killer?" Teagan asked, keeping one eye on the news report. Her expression showed a hint of frustration as the day's events threatened to keep her away from her children.

"The police determined that two of the victims were killed with the same type of gun," President Sanders revealed.

Teagan pressed her fingers to her temples. "Give me a few days to review everything and get back to you."

"Teagan, I need to know you'll take the case," President Sanders insisted. "We've had enough bad press over the past few months, and catching this person quickly would help me out."

A visiting foreign leader and a serial killer on the same day? Something was off. She wanted to say no but knew she couldn't let someone else take the lead on this case.

Teagan's shoulders slumped. "We're on it, Sir."

"Thank you, Agent Red," President Sanders said before ending the call.

Teagan switched her mindset from her director role to agent on the job. Closing her eyes, she recalled Sean's recent death. He'd devoted his life to protecting Teagan and her family, and he'd taken a bullet to save her life. She never wanted to experience that pain again, and her sole focus moving forward was to keep her team safe.

"Call the guys. We meet in thirty minutes. I need to shower and check a few things." Teagan picked up the landline to let her husband know she was going to miss lunch. Therapy sessions had worked wonders to bring them closer over the past year, and she'd promised to make their relationship a priority unless she was out of the country.

A blush tickled up the back of her neck. "Hey, honey."

"It's not even seven a.m.," Christian grumbled.

Teagan laughed. "Sorry. I got a call."

"It's bad, isn't it?"

"Not sure yet."

"The kids wanted you to drop them off at school today," Christian reminded her.

"I know. I planned to be home before they woke up, but the president called me."

"Keep me updated. Love you."

"Give my babies a kiss for me." Teagan ended the call.

She stared at the TV screen showing the vice president greeting Minister Fernsby at the airport. Grabbing the report, she turned up the volume.

"Minister of Defense Penny Fernsby is here to discuss how to move forward with security," the GNS reporter informed.

Teagan took in the crowd surrounding the airport, noticing a familiar figure as the minister and vice president walked toward the waiting limo.

"Why is Congressman Wilde at the minister's greeting?" Teagan murmured to herself.

Shutting off the TV, she strolled to her bathroom to shower and change. Thirty minutes later, she grabbed the file from her desk, locked her office, and headed to the conference room to discuss the potential serial killer. It was unusual not to have the FBI investigating a serial killer, but the president had specifically requested Teagan and her team.

She needed answers for him by the end of the day.

Chapter Two

His brow furrowed as he looked down the scope of the rifle, and sweat dripped into his eye. His stomach was twisted in knots as he wiped his forehead on the back of his sleeve. The timeline of his next kill wasn't ideal, but he had no other choice.

Sunlight blasted his body as he lay on the rooftop. Loud music blared from cars, covering the noise of the crowd. He'd waited a few weeks to take out his next victim and wanted to ensure things went without a hitch. Wrapping his index finger around the trigger, he closed his eyes and whispered a prayer as he took the shot.

Panic erupted as people scrambled for cover, but his job was done. He disassembled the rifle and hurriedly packed up, removing his gloves and slipping on his shades. Strolling to the rooftop exit, he descended the stairs and blended with the crowd. Sirens blared, but they were too late. The victim was dead on the concrete with a hole between his eyes.

"Someone call the police!" a woman screamed as he jogged to his beat-up Toyota Corolla.

He threw his bag in the back, slid behind the wheel, and took off. He smiled as the ambulance and fire truck passed him. Merging onto the freeway, he turned up the radio to listen to the news report as he headed back to Queens.

"*Kendra, this is the third shooting in New York. President Sanders has now commented. Let's listen,*" Cami of Eighty-Nine Radio News and Sports reported.

"*The governor and citizens of New York have my full support. We will do everything in our power to catch the people or persons behind these crimes,*" President Sanders stated.

He pulled the car into an alley on a deserted street two blocks from his home. Removing his gear, he covered the car with a worn blanket and walked home.

"Jeff, where have you been?" his wife, Claire, demanded, her cheeks red with frustration.

"I had to work," he replied, stepping around her.

"Did you get my text message?"

Her hard stare followed his every move. Ignoring her pout had become routine lately.

Jeff headed to the locked basement door and removed his keys. "Sorry, I was busy."

"We need groceries for dinner," Claire fussed, following behind him.

He turned to face her. "I'll go grab what we need in a few minutes."

Claire scanned his attire, looking at the bag in his hand. "How? My car isn't working, and yours is in the shop. Did Bert drive you home?"

"Yeah."

"That's funny."

"What's funny?"

"I called Bert, and he said you two haven't talked in months," Claire challenged.

He hadn't factored in Claire contacting Bert. "He and I had a falling out over a bet, but we're good now."

"So, you were gambling again after you promised you wouldn't," she accused, stomping off to the kitchen.

Annoyed by her nagging, Jeff continued to the basement, shutting the door behind him and throwing the deadbolt. Flicking on the light, he marched down the stairs and dropped his bag on the table. He grabbed the remote to turn on the TV, smiling as he listened to the news about the latest shooting. His gaze fell on the list of names he still needed to cross off. Remaining in the basement to avoid dinner with his wife, he planned his next mission.

* * *

They'd been in the conference room for an hour when the president called. Things had escalated fast, and he'd demanded they take over the case from the local police.

Teagan listened to Broderick read over the reports of the latest shooting in Times Square. "One male killed by a headshot."

"What are the odds of two bodies within twenty-four hours?" Teagan asked, fiddling with the pen in her hand.

"Are you thinking there's more than one perpetrator?" Gregory's blue eyes stretched wide.

Teagan leaned an arm across the back of the chair and crossed her legs. "Feels like escalation. Panic."

Broderick's eyes narrowed on the computer screen. "True. Maybe something rattled them."

Daughtrey folded his arms over his chest. "I can head

out to the scene and check with some of the business owners."

"Take Broderick with you," Teagan instructed.

Broderick changed the screen to the replay of the French minister of defense with the vice president.

"I saw this earlier," Gregory recalled.

Broderick stood, passing around documentation of the visit. "They need extra security on their detail."

Teagan grimaced as she stretched her stiff limbs. "Why wasn't I made aware of this visit?"

Usually, Spider kept her updated. Broderick obtaining the information seemed suspicious.

"Your assistant was on a call, and you weren't around," Broderick muttered, staring at Teagan.

Studying the scheduled events for Minister Fernsby, Teagan surmised that the president was aware and had held back from telling her.

"Minister Fernsby is here for a week, but they have security," Spider commented.

"I agree, but it's coming from the higher-ups," Broderick insisted.

"We're dealing with a serial killer in New York. Adding around-the-clock security would stretch us thin," Teagan pointed out as she dialed the White House.

The agents fell quiet as Teagan waited to speak to the president. She covered the receiver with her hand. "Broderick, you and Daughtrey scope out the last shooting location while Spider and I head to the UN offices. I see Minister Fernsby has a meeting set up in an hour."

Broderick and Daughtrey jumped up to leave. Gregory took the case file and headed back to his office. Teagan perched on the edge of the table as Spider walked around to face her.

"Director Stone, I already know why you're calling," President Sanders spoke before Teagan could greet him.

Concern pinched her voice. "Mr. President, I don't like to be blindsided."

"My intent was to keep you and the team away from certain situations, but the vice president informed me that Minister Fernsby insisted on having you on her detail while she's here."

"Why?" Teagan challenged.

"She's a fan of your work."

"Sir, I'm no celebrity. I'm just doing my job. I have bigger issues than running after Minister Fernsby to ensure she gets to a party on time."

"Teagan," he cajoled.

She sighed. He knew she always gave in when he used her first name. "Okay, but I need complete control of Minister Fernsby's movements so I can focus on this murder case you've dropped in my lap."

"Done," President Sanders replied.

"Okay. I can meet her in thirty minutes."

"She'll be waiting," the president responded.

Teagan thanked him and ended the call, blowing out a resigned breath.

"Two cases?" Spider questioned.

Teagan rubbed her tired eyes. "Yep. A serial killer and a minister of defense visiting the city."

Spider turned to leave the room. "May as well sleep here for the next few nights."

"Sleep? What's that?" Teagan grunted, grabbing the case files and heading to her office.

She was answering a few emails when her assistant, Celine, knocked and entered.

"Director Stone, here's your breakfast." Celine placed

coffee, fruit, and a muffin from the local cafe on her desk. "And you have messages from your husband and kids."

"Thank you, but I'm heading out for an early meeting. I'll call my family in the car." Teagan lifted the coffee and took a sip.

"Sure, no problem. Do you need me to order lunch for you?"

"I'll let you know. I'll be gone for most of the day, so hold my calls," Teagan said as she strolled from her office with her coffee.

Teagan joined Spider and Gregory at the elevator as Broderick, and Daughtrey passed by. "Try not to get in trouble, gentlemen."

"Promise." Daughtrey threw his hand in the air.

"They're lying," Gregory quipped.

"I know." Teagan strode onto the elevator as Spider pressed the button.

The doors opened for garage parking as Jason, her new detail, finished loading the car. He'd been with them since Sean's death, and the kids loved him. She was grateful for how quickly they'd adjusted.

Teagan slid into the back seat of the Escalade with Spider while Gregory sat in the passenger seat next to Jason.

"Where to, Director Stone?" Jason asked.

"Please, call me Teagan, and we're going to the UN offices."

"UN offices, Director Stone." Jason put the car in reverse and backed out of the reserved spot.

The security gates opened, and Jason drove into traffic. Laying her coffee in the cup holder, Teagan pulled her cell from her pocket to call home.

"Hi, Mommy," Tatum answered the house phone.

Teagan grinned. "Tatum, what did I tell you about answering the phone?"

"Um, I forgot," Tatum giggled.

Teagan shook her head. "Where's your dad?"

"Dad!" Tatum yelled. Teagan winced and pulled the phone from her ear. "When are you coming home?"

"Soon as I get through with my meetings, Tatum. Be good at school."

"Teagan?" Christian came on the phone.

"Hey. Celine told me you and the kids called." She stared out the window at the increasing traffic as they approached the UN offices, noting the protests en route. Getting to Forty-Sixth Street was chaotic with the mid-morning traffic.

"Yeah, I wanted to say hi, but you'll be home for dinner, right?"

"Of course. I'll do my best to wrap up as soon as possible."

"Great. Tatum, say bye to your mom."

"Bye, Mom!" Tatum shouted in the background.

"That girl," Teagan chuckled.

"Like mother, like daughter," Christian laughed.

Teagan promised to be home for dinner before ending the call. The radio played her favorite old-school music, from Aretha Franklin to Marvin Gaye, while she took in the city.

Teagan's thoughts strayed to the murder victims. She couldn't help thinking that something else was brewing.

Chapter Three

Jason parked in the reserved section of the UN building, and they made their way through the crowd.

"Murder! Stop the war!" the protestors screamed, waving placards and recording on their cell phones.

Teagan flashed her badge at one of the security guards.

"Keep going." He waved them through, and they entered the building.

Teagan scanned the crowd, memorizing as many faces as possible. She glanced up at the ceiling and surveyed the lobby. "Cameras outside, correct?"

"Yeah. Twenty-four hours," the guard replied.

Teagan nodded toward the crowd outside as she marched toward the elevator. "Spider, we need names with faces."

"Already on it," Spider said, removing his cell phone.

Teagan paused as she spotted Minister of Defense Penny Fernsby and Congressman Koen Wilde deep in conversation. They were standing close to each other, and Teagan's eyes narrowed at the look that passed between them.

She'd seen the congressman at the airport with the vice president, and his being here raised red flags.

Congressman Wilde's frown disappeared and was replaced with a smile as he noticed Teagan. "Director Stone, nice to see you again." He stuck out his hand.

"Congressman Wilde," Teagan acknowledged, shaking his hand firmly. "I'm surprised to see you here."

He chuckled. "I have to admit, when the president explained the visit, I wanted to come for personal reasons."

"Personal?" Teagan arched her brow.

"Director Stone, I've been a long-time admirer of your work," Minister Fernsby interrupted, extending her hand.

Teagan shook it. "I was surprised when you requested me for your detail."

"Sorry for the last-minute change, but I wanted the best," the minister replied.

Congressman Wilde gestured to the open conference room. "Perhaps we should talk in here."

"After you, Congressman Wilde." Teagan followed them inside.

Spider closed the door behind them, and Teagan sat at the table facing the door. Minister Fernsby sat at the head of the conference table.

"Why are you here, Congressman?" Teagan asked bluntly.

"I'm Minister Fernsby's host. We've been working closely to reduce cyberattacks and human trafficking."

Minister Fernsby straightened her shoulders. "As I explained to Congressman Wilde, we need to strengthen our relationships and focus our spending on cutting off terrorists before they strike."

"In case you're unaware, we're dealing with a serial killer in New York," Teagan said. Arranging twenty-four-seven protection for the minister while trying to catch a serial killer was becoming more problematic by the minute.

Congressman Wilde nodded. "I heard. Any leads?"

Teagan glanced at Minister Fernsby. "No, which is why I wasn't prepared to be on the detail for your visit."

"My workload shouldn't be too heavy. I only have three outings in the city," Minister Fernsby confirmed.

"Those will need to be canceled unless we can get inside the buildings to check them over," Teagan pointed out.

"These plans have been in place for months."

"I'm sorry, but in order to do my job effectively, I need complete control of your schedule," Teagan challenged.

Minister Fernsby looked at Congressman Wilde and then back at Teagan. "I agree."

Teagan rose and shook hands with Minister Fernsby and Congressman Wilde, ready to get home and see her family. "I'll have my team escort you from the building."

"I can't leave yet. I have a conference call scheduled with the vice president."

Teagan patted her pocket for her phone. "Where are you staying?"

"At the Arlo Hotel." Minister Fernsby watched as Teagan made notes on her phone.

"My guys will come with you and check your room. The conference call can be rescheduled. We need to finalize your schedule," Teagan said as they left the office.

Minister Fernsby gestured to the office down the hall. "I'd rather not keep the vice president waiting."

"I can assure you that the vice president will understand." Teagan held the elevator as Fernsby grabbed her things, observing her with Congressman Wilde. "Check on Wilde," Teagan murmured to Spider.

"Even his sponsored bills?" he asked.

Teagan nodded and called Jason to be ready with the car. The shouts of the protestors seemed louder than ever as they exited the UN building.

"Stay behind me," she instructed Minister Fernsby.

Reporters shouted questions at the French minister as Teagan walked ahead of her. Spider covered her back, and Minister Fernsby's security flanked her on either side.

"Keep your head down," Teagan said, shoving people out of the way as she moved swiftly through the crowd.

She yanked the door open, and Minister Fernsby climbed inside with Congressman Wilde. Teagan's gaze fell on a young woman wearing black running toward the car, holding a sign to abolish foreign partnerships.

"Let's go!" Spider shouted, shutting the door, and Jason sped through the traffic.

"Anything stick out to you?" Spider turned in his seat to face Teagan.

"No, but we need to know why so many people were waving signs demanding Minister Fernsby's death." Teagan glanced at the minister. "Care to tell us why you're really here?"

Minister Fernsby shrugged. "I'm a politician. People hate politicians. Like you, I have enemies."

"There's a difference between killing people for a living and saving people for a living," Teagan quipped.

Congressman Wilde glowered at Teagan. Not one to be intimidated, she returned his glare. She sat back in her seat as they headed for the hotel, considering extra security for Minister Fernsby now that she'd seen the protestors' reactions.

Fifteen minutes later, they arrived at the Arlo Hotel. Jason jumped out to open the door for Teagan and Minister Fernsby while Spider encouraged Congressman Wilde to stay in the car.

"You're leaving me here?" the congressman asked in disbelief.

"The less people we have to worry about, the better." Spider pointed at the second SUV behind them, carrying Minister Fernsby's security team.

Teagan ignored them and escorted the minister through the hotel doors to the elevator. "Which floor?"

"Suite," Minister Fernsby corrected, removing her key card as the elevator rose smoothly.

The doors opened, and her guards checked that the area was clear before leading them to her room.

"Clear," one of the guards announced once they'd checked the suite.

"You have fifteen minutes to change and gather what you need," Teagan said, checking the room herself.

Minister Fernsby nodded and went into her bedroom to gather her things.

"What are you thinking?" Spider asked quietly, keeping an eye on the minister and her team.

"She's hiding something," Teagan replied.

"Agreed," Spider responded.

Minister Fernsby looked agitated as she stalked into the living room. "How long will I need to be at your offices?"

Time slowed as the flash of a gun muzzle caught Teagan's eye. She reacted instinctively, reaching for her gun.

"Get down!" she yelled, running toward Minister Fernsby.

Bullets hit the window, shattering it.

"Teagan!" Spider shouted.

The minister's guards dropped, one after another.

"Stay down!" she hissed.

"Oh, my God!" Fernsby screamed.

Teagan stumbled, reaching into her pocket for her phone to call for backup.

Spider crawled to the guards, checking their pulses as more glass shattered.

"Don't move." Teagan reached the wall and leaned to look out the window as more gunshots ricocheted through the suite.

"Teagan!" Jason busted into the suite, his eyes falling on Fernsby, Teagan, and Spider huddled in the corner.

The gunfire ceased, and Teagan suspected the gunman was reloading.

"Stay low. Go with Jason," she muttered to Minister Fernsby.

Teagan and Spider followed, making a beeline for the door as hotel security arrived. She flashed her badge at the burly guard. "Agent Stone, in charge of Minister Fernsby's security on behalf of the president. Secure the room until our investigation team arrives."

Teagan dialed Daughtrey as she followed Jason and Minister Fernsby to the elevator. "Are you still at the location?" she demanded as soon as he answered.

"We're heading back to the office now."

"No, meet us at the Arlo Hotel."

"Near the UN offices?"

"Yes. We have a situation."

"On our way." Daughtrey hung up.

Teagan's heart was still pounding as she pressed the button for the hotel lobby.

Chapter Four

Cursing to himself for missing the open shot, he quickly packed up his equipment, looking at the dead housekeeper on the floor. Her death hadn't been part of the plan, but she'd been in the way when he'd needed to get in closer range of his target.

Zipping up his jacket and removing the "Do not disturb" sign, he placed it on the door handle. He pulled his hat low over his eyes and sauntered to the fire exit stairs to avoid security cameras.

Coming here had been a risk after his earlier kill. He needed to get home quickly.

He exited the stairs into the alley, scanning to ensure it was empty before walking to the main street and climbing into his car. As he pulled away, he checked his rearview to see the police, FBI, and DEA surrounding the hotel.

"Not much longer." Jeff grinned, turning up the radio to listen to his favorite sports channel.

He clenched the steering wheel, knowing he'd have to readjust his timetable to take out his target. His wife didn't know why he'd lost his job. He'd had dreams of being successful in his field, but outside forces had snatched it all away. People employed behind him had been promoted. He'd tried to talk to his boss about getting his job back, but his calls and emails went unanswered. Revenge was the only way people would take notice.

He parked the car in the same spot two blocks away, concealing it under the worn blanket before treading down the street to his home. The TV was blaring as he entered through the back door. He grabbed a beer from the fridge, flipped off the top, and gulped it down.

"Breaking news. We're receiving reports that the French minister of defense has been the victim of an assassination attempt," the GNS news reporter announced.

"Can you believe this?" Claire asked over her shoulder. "People are crazy nowadays."

Jeff grunted. "Probably had a reason."

She scowled at his response. "You're kidding, right?"

He ignored her question. "Did you cook?"

Claire turned the volume down. "People are dying because of some crazed man."

He turned to head to the basement. "Not our problem."

Claire rose from the couch and followed him. "Where did you go?"

He paused, glaring at her. "What did you say?"

"I asked where you were."

"Looking for a job."

Something in Claire's heart told her he was lying, but she wanted to trust him and get their marriage back on track. They'd been together for fifteen years, high school sweethearts. They'd promised to travel the world together, have kids, and be the stars in each other's family and friend groups. But their dreams had unraveled when she got hurt at work.

Jeff noticed Claire's attitude shifting when she went on disability. Then the money stopped as funds changed with the requirements of reapplying. All the bills landed on her shoulders once he got fired, and bitterness sat in her voice each time she saw him. So when he'd lied about how he'd lost his job, her disappointment in their relationship had hardened her heart.

"I think we should talk with someone," Claire suggested.

"No."

"No?" Her cheeks turned red at his tone.

"There's nothing wrong with our marriage. I'll have a job in a few days. Get off my back, Claire." Jeff stomped away.

He had bigger plans. If he couldn't do the job he'd done before, no job would do. Claire had to get on board, or he'd show her what he was capable of.

Jeff unlocked the basement door and slipped inside. Placing his things on the table, he grabbed the remote and switched on the TV. Pulling the map from his bag, he smirked as he circled the points of his kill shots. In desperation, he pushed the boundary and set forth on a journey he knew would only lead to jail or death. It was naive to think he'd get his job back. So now he was content to go out with a bang.

"Three down, and we have little to go on at this time," the GNS reporter said. *"The Arlo Hotel is the scene of an attempt on Minister Fernsby's life."*

He watched as the scene played out on the TV.

Gunfire rang out, and people scrambled in shock, running for protection.

"Get inside!" voices shouted, sprinting to shelter in doorways, behind cars, and in surrounding buildings.

"Now we have footage from the UN offices a few minutes before the minister left."

Angry mobs yelled and screamed at Minister Fernsby, Teagan, and the team. Jeff wanted to cause more problems. Maybe he would. Hitting her at the Arlo Hotel was the goal, and he knew she'd likely be transferred to another location.

Picking up his phone, he scrolled through his email and saw the schedule of events for the week. The opera would be the next stop. He could take them out in one hit.

Finishing his beer, he wiped his hands and packed up the map. He went back upstairs to eat before showering. He left his door unlocked, figuring Claire wouldn't go into the basement since he'd demanded she stay out of his private space.

While Jeff was in the shower, Claire went into the kitchen, shaking her head when she saw his empty plate in the sink. Realizing she wasn't married to the same man she'd met in high school had awakened her need for answers. Was he cheating on her? Why had he really lost his job?

As she left the kitchen, she saw the basement door was ajar. Perhaps she could discover what her husband had been up to after all.

Quietly pushing the door open, she ran her hand over the wall to find the light switch before descending the stairs. At the bottom, she saw a TV on a stand and a table with papers scattered across the surface.

Bam.

Claire jumped at the slamming of the door. She

swiveled to see Jeff at the top of the stairs wearing clean pants and a shirt.

"What are you doing down here?"

Claire stuttered, "Um-I-I-just wanted to know what you've been up to."

"None of your business, Claire."

"Jeff, you spend all your time down here. I never see you. Are you seeing someone?"

Jeff slipped his hand into his pocket, removed a pair of black gloves, and slid them on. "You know, Claire, I really wanted to make this work," he said, advancing on her slowly.

Claire's eyes widened, and the knot of anxiety in her stomach grew. "We do work. We just need counseling."

Jeff clenched his fists as he stepped off the last stair and moved to stand in front of her. Caressing her cheek, he stared into her eyes. Then he moved his hands to her throat.

"We will never work." He tightened his grip around her neck, squeezing while she gasped for air. She fought him, pummeling his chest and trying to scratch his face. Jeff dodged her blows to avoid injury.

"You should have stayed out of the basement, Claire."

* * *

Jeff got rid of his wife's body and replaced his car with an Oldsmobile for sale down the street. After replacing the license plate and fixing a few things, he was ready to take the trip into the city for the opera.

Watching the news reports, he'd seen Minister Fernsby working out of the UN offices with close protection. Her plans to fly to D.C. to meet with the president were canceled, and only a select few knew her daily activities. Usually, she jogged in the morning, but she was limiting her movements to business matters only until she left the country.

Arriving at his destination, Jeff parked the car a few blocks from where Minister Fernsby and her team would be arriving. Taking his things out of the car, he surveyed the area and hurried toward the building in the theater district. Minister Fernsby was expected at St. James Theatre within the hour, and Jeff climbed the stairs, heading to the roof and away from people. Pushing the door open, he lugged his bag on his shoulder to the edge of the building. Pulling out his gun, he locked everything into place and lined up the best position through his scope.

Police sirens blared, and he swallowed, wiping the sweat from his brow. Doors opening. Camera flashes. He lost concentration, and his trigger finger jerked, sending a shot into the air.

"Shit!" he hissed.

All hell broke loose as security shoved everybody back, and police officers jumped from their cars.

"Anyone got eyes on the shooter?" someone yelled.

Jeff couldn't wait any longer. He aimed and fired at the stretch limo and black escalade lined up out front.

"Up there!" someone screamed.

He dropped to the ground, breathing hard. Scrambling, he disassembled the rifle, placed it in his bag, and removed his gloves. He paused halfway down the first flight of stairs, knowing they'd come this way. Taking the next exit door, he pulled his hat low and blended with a group of tourists.

"We have to see the Empire State Building before we

leave," one of the tourists said, holding up a map of attractions.

"Tomorrow. We have all day. I'm excited for Chicago on Broadway," her companion replied.

Staying behind the group as the elevator doors dinged, he turned his face away as police officers rushed down the halls.

"We need everyone to quietly head to their rooms," one of the officers instructed.

Jeff slipped to the back of the group and back into the stairwell, taking the exit to the next floor.

"Did you need help?" Jeff offered an elderly couple struggling with their bags of shopping.

"Oh, thank you so much," the elderly woman replied, letting him take the large grocery bags from her hands.

Chapter Five

Three hours before the shooting Minister Penny Fernsby had been moved to a different hotel. She poured the wine as Congressman Koen Wilde removed his coat and laid it on the couch. She held out the glass to him, and he took it before tangling his fingers with hers and pressing a kiss to her forehead. She wrapped her arms around his neck and stood on tiptoes to capture his lips.

"How are you feeling?" Wilde asked.

"Good, now we're alone."

"I can't stay long."

"Why not?"

He moved away and went to stand in front of the window, looking out at the city. "We shouldn't be seen together."

"We have the opera tonight."

"Maybe we should cancel."

Penny sighed. "Is this about me not agreeing to the deal?"

"I put in a lot of time and negotiated with a lot of people to make this deal happen."

"How is that my problem?"

He jerked his head around. "Cutting those costs will lead to more money than we've ever seen."

Rubbing her forehead, she paced back and forth. "I trusted you and came here to be with you."

Koen moved toward her and clasped her hands. "Get the deal signed, and we can talk about us later."

Fernsby snatched her hands away. "You've been using me. None of this was real, Koen," she said, waving a hand between them.

Koen gulped the remainder of his wine and grabbed his coat. "I have a previous engagement."

Penny frowned. "You're not coming to the opera tonight?"

"No. It would be too risky to be seen together."

"We were seen together at the UN offices and Arlo Hotel."

"That's different. It was business."

"Why do I get the feeling you're breaking up with me?"

"Penny, you're not thinking rationally. Once you sign the agreement, we can be open about our relationship and how we feel about each other." Koen ran his hands down her arms.

"And if I don't agree to the terms?"

"Let's not think about what could go wrong. We both need to be on the same page."

Penny sighed. "Fine. I'll see you later tonight after the opera?"

"Maybe."

"Come on, Koen. You promised."

"I need to wrap a few things up before I fly back to D.C."

"Meet me tonight, Koen." Penny glowered.

"We'll see, Penny."

Koen left her room and stepped onto the elevator. Jumping into a relationship with Penny Fernsby hadn't been his best idea. He liked spending time with her, but his goal had been financial gain. When they'd met a year ago, he'd recognized how beneficial she could be for his career. He'd spent time learning about her, sitting in on meetings when she visited, and eventually charmed her into a relationship. She'd become a pawn in his plans to secure a ten-million-dollar deal, if he could persuade her to cut costs on multiple French trade deals.

Riding in the back of the car, Koen arranged to move his flight up to get back to D.C. He was reluctant to end his week at the UN offices for Penny's speech, but he needed to show his support to ensure she signed off on his plans.

Back at his hotel room, he switched on the news and ordered room service as he read over the bill proposal Penny needed to sign.

A knock at the door was followed by a male voice. "Housekeeping."

Koen dropped the papers on the table and stalked to the door. The door flew back as he opened it, and a masked man barged inside.

Koen screamed. "What the...?"

A gun with a silencer pressed against his temple as the intruder shut the door behind him. "I've been waiting to do this for a long time."

"Who are you?"

"Won't matter to you for much longer."

"Another shooting occurred at St. James Theater just as Minister of Defense Fernsby arrived." The CGN news reporter's voice drifted to them from the TV.

Koen's eyes widened as he looked at the masked man. "It's you." He stumbled back with his hands up. "I have money. Take whatever you want."

"Your money is worthless to me," the intruder sneered.

One shot between the eyes, and Congressman Koen Wilde dropped to the ground. Wasting no time, the masked man stepped from the room and pushed the housekeeping cart down the hallway. He unlocked the closet door and shoved the cart inside with the dead security guard.

"Thank you for your service to our country."

Chuckling, he strolled to the emergency exit.

* * *

Teagan paced in front of the outline of Congressman Wilde's body. People were dying, and no one had answers.

"Where is he?" Minister Fernsby tried to enter the room.

A police officer held her back. "Ma'am, it's a crime scene."

"I need to see him!" The minister's voice was shrill as she yanked herself from his hold.

Teagan marched over to her. "Why are you here, Minister Fernsby?"

"Penny. My name is Penny," she said numbly, looking at the markings on the floor.

Teagan's voice softened. "Why are you here, Penny?"

"Because he's..." Her voice trailed off, and she shook her head.

"He's what?"

"I loved him," Penny gasped.

"You were dating?"

Penny nodded. "We've been together for six months."

"Why hide it?"

"He wanted to keep our relationship a secret. I made him promise to go public after my speech at the UN later this week."

Teagan sighed. "I knew something odd was going on when he showed up to greet you at the airport."

"We talked yesterday before the opera."

"Wait. You saw him before the opera?" Spider asked.

Penny walked over to the couch and sank down on it. "He came to see me, and I begged him to come with me, but he said he had a prior engagement. I should have called him after the attempted shooting last night, but I was exhausted and fell asleep."

Teagan sat in the chair opposite. "What did you discuss when you saw him before the opera?"

"I told him I suspected he was using me to sign off on his sponsored bill."

"Money," Broderick remarked, holding up Koen's phone.

Penny lifted her eyes to him. "At first, I didn't want to believe it, but I had a gut feeling that everything would change once I signed my name."

"His social media has a few death threats." Broderick walked over to Teagan with the phone.

"Gregory, download everything from his computers and phone. I want it all, from his favorite coffee to the store where he buys his suits," Teagan commanded.

"Someone takes a shot at you at the opera, and an hour later, Congressman Wilde is murdered in his hotel room," Spider murmured.

"Gather your things, Penny. You're coming with us." Teagan motioned for her team to escort Penny from the room.

"What are you thinking?" Spider inquired.

Teagan grimaced. "Same as you. That Koen Wilde was the target all along."

* * *

Two hours later, Teagan sat in the briefing room on a video call with the pathologist in charge of Congressman Wilde's case. Broderick, Spider, and Daughtrey were also present, along with Gregory, who was still accessing Koen's information.

Teagan sat forward in her chair. "Dr. Grant, thank you for making this case a priority."

Dr. Chandler Grant adjusted his glasses as he clicked through the photos of Koen's body on the screen.

"One kill shot between the eyes. This is consistent with the other murders. In my opinion, he knew the killer."

"Anything else?" Teagan asked.

"No defensive wounds, which suggests he was taken by surprise."

"Thank you, Dr. Grant. We'll be in touch if we have more questions." Teagan ended the video call.

Spider snapped his fingers as he examined each photo of the four murders.

Broderick studied the crime scenes. "You got something?"

"They all worked for Congressman Wilde," Spider muttered.

"Why didn't we know this before?" Teagan asked, glaring at her team.

"We didn't have time to investigate before we got pulled onto Fernsby's security detail," Daughtrey pointed out.

Teagan knew that blaming her team wouldn't make the situation better. She needed to take a step back and get a clear mindset. Like them, she hadn't had much time to sit with all the details, and now a US Congressman was dead.

Teagan needed to get the team on the same page, and Penny Fernsby needed to be moved to a safe location.

"Let's go. We'll take the back streets."

* * *

They escorted Penny Fernsby to the waiting vehicle. Daughtrey held the door open for Teagan and Penny to get in the back seat, he and Broderick got in behind them, and Spider sat up front with Jason.

Penny Fernsby huddled in the corner of the car with her cell phone. She was reading Koen Wilde's last text messages about announcing their relationship. Guilt ate away at her over Koen's death. She wished they hadn't parted the way they had.

Jason navigated the backstreets before stopping

behind an identical black escalade. Teagan jumped out of the vehicle and helped Penny transfer into the other car.

"What about my stuff at the hotel?" Penny asked.

"Don't worry. Your possessions will be returned to you once you reach your new location."

Teagan returned to the vehicle with the guys and watched the other car speed off with Minister Fernsby.

Chapter Six

The repercussions of Congressman Wilde's death weighed heavily on Teagan, and she barely slept. The late-night news channels replayed the events and discussed waning national security.

Teagan got up early and took a quick shower. She'd gotten home late last night, but at least she'd managed to have dinner with her family.

Christian was sitting on the bed when she strolled from the bathroom. "Did you see the news?" he asked, indicating the TV screen.

Teagan grabbed a pair of pants and a shirt. "Not yet. I have to fly out of town. I have a meeting with the president."

"They're saying France is upset about what's going on."

Tegan slipped on her shoes. "Christian, you know I can't get into details."

"Whatever is going on could lead to a bigger problem for both countries. Should I be worried?"

She looped her arms around Christian's neck, and he

placed his hands on her hips. "My job is to protect you and the kids. I will do everything in my power to make sure it doesn't come to that."

She believed she could prevent World War Three, but she knew men in charge with large egos would do what they wanted at the end of the day.

"Mommy!" Cole burst into their room.

"Cole, what did I tell you about knocking before you enter a bedroom?" Teagan sat on her husband's lap.

"Um, that everyone deserves privacy? Sorry, but I wanted to make sure you remembered," Cole said, holding out a piece of paper.

Teagan scanned the paper. "What's this?"

"My field trip to the museum."

Teagan bent to hug him. "I forgot, baby."

"You promised to come since Dad went last time." Cole poked his lip out.

Teagan sighed. "You're right."

"Are you going to be able to come?" Cole asked.

Cupping his chin, she pressed a kiss on his forehead. "Yes, Cole. Don't worry."

"Come on. Let's go eat breakfast." Christian patted Cole on the shoulder as they left the bedroom.

Tatum and CJ were eating pancakes and drinking orange juice in the kitchen.

Teagan kissed their heads and moved to the counter to pour herself a cup of coffee from the pot.

"Are you staying for breakfast?" Tatum's brown eyes pleaded with her.

"I am."

"Can we have a girl's day? Please?" Tatum pressed her palms together in a prayer position.

Christian raised his eyebrows at Teagan.

"I'm sorry, guys. Work was supposed to get easier, but my load has gotten tougher," Teagan explained.

"You're the boss, Mom. We know you can't be here for everything," CJ remarked.

"True. But I need to put in more boundaries. I'm going to change that right now."

Christian frowned. "What do you mean?"

"Spider and the Team can go to D.C. I'll stay here with the kids."

"Teagan, hold on. I know you feel like you haven't been around lately, but your work is important," Christian said, reaching for her hand.

Tatum nodded. "Daddy's right, Mom. We know your job is important."

"The most important thing to me is you guys. I'll let the President know I won't be there," Teagan said, grabbing the house phone.

Having a team behind her meant she could delegate. She had to relinquish control and let them do their jobs. Spider could handle himself with President Sanders, and even though she and Broderick weren't the best of friends, she trusted that he knew what was at stake.

Spider picked up, and Teagan explained the situation, letting him know she wouldn't be going to D.C.

"Taking Broderick could cause problems with President Sanders," Spider pointed out.

"He'll understand. I need this time with my family. It's personal, Spider."

"All right. I trust your judgment."

"Take the jet to D.C. I want an update before the night is over," Teagan instructed.

"Copy, Boss."

"And have Gregory research the other leaders on the bill."

"Are we interviewing them?" Spider probed.

Teagan sat at the table and cut into the plate of pancakes Christian placed in front of her. "Maybe. But now we know the connection leads to Wilde, it might not be necessary."

"I'm sending everything to your inbox."

"Thanks, and have Celine move all my meetings for today and tomorrow."

Spider joked. "Mom duty."

Teagan smiled as she looked at her family. "Always."

"Cole, get your things together. We're going to the museum," Teagan said as soon as she ended the call.

Cole beamed. "Yes! Thanks, Mom." He jumped up and ran off to grab his backpack.

Laughing at their middle child, Christian winked at his wife, and she blew him a kiss.

"Tatum, we'll have a girl's day tomorrow, honey. Is that okay?"

"Yes, Mom," Tatum answered.

"Thanks, baby. CJ, what's going on in your world?"

"Nothing much. I might have a girlfriend," he teased.

"Girlfriend?" Teagan choked on her coffee, and Christian jumped up to pat her on the back.

Laughing, CJ waved a hand dismissively. "Joking, Mom."

Teagan poked his arm. "Boy, don't scare me like that."

Tatum and Christian laughed at their interaction as Cole ran back into the kitchen.

Teagan stood and picked up her purse, tucking the permission slip inside as they headed for the front door.

"Call me if you two need anything." Christian held

the door open, and Cole ran out to the black SUV where Jason stood waiting.

"Are you good with taking CJ and Tatum to school?" Teagan asked Christian.

"Yeah. I know this field trip meant a lot to Cole," Christian said, watching Cole jump in the back of the car.

Teagan kissed her husband. "Call me if you need me to grab anything for dinner."

"We'll be fine. Just focus on Cole."

Teagan slid into the back seat and helped Cole with his seatbelt. She put her phone on silent, sat back, and listened to her son talk about how much fun he was going to have with his friends.

* * *

Teagan held Cole's hand, listening to him describe all the different dinosaurs. His class had the entire place to themselves. Cole ran to his best friend, Guster, pointing at the *Triceratops* skeleton. Teagan stood off to the side with another mom, watching the kids interact.

The tour guide came over to direct the rest of the group to assemble. "That's one of the last-known non-avian dinosaurs," she explained.

"Wow!" all the kids said in unison.

"Exciting, right?" she asked before explaining the different dinosaurs.

Cole gestured to his mom. "Mom, look at this!"

"I see, Cole." Teagan waved at him. Her phone vibrated in her pocket, and she stepped away to answer it. "Agent Stone."

"Agent Stone, please tell me why my minister of

defense is down at the police station under suspicion of murder?" a man with a French accent asked.

"Who am I speaking with?"

"Prime Minister of France, Beau Perly."

Teagan looked at the crowd of kids moving to the next display down the hall.

"Prime Minister Perly, I think you're mistaken."

Beau Perly hissed, "Please don't insult my intelligence."

"My team is on their way to talk with President Sanders as we speak."

"I've been a longtime ally of the United States, Agent Stone. I'd hate to make this into something more."

"What are you trying to say?"

"Teagan, this is President Sanders. You're on a three-way secure line," President Sanders said, joining the conversation.

Teagan froze.

"You have my apologies, Prime Minister Perly. I assure you we will fix the situation with Minister of Defense Fernsby," President Sanders continued.

Cole ran over and grabbed her arm. "Mom, come on."

"I'm sorry, Agent Stone. Are we interrupting you?" Prime Minister Perly asked sarcastically. "Is something more important than my minister of defense being in a US jail?"

Covering the speaker, Teagan grasped Cole's shoulder. "Honey, I'm right behind you. Go with your friends."

"Agent Stone is our best, Prime Minister Perly," President Sanders assured him.

"You have twenty-four hours," Prime Minister Perly snapped.

"Is that a threat?" Teagan demanded.

"I don't make threats, Agent Stone. I suggest you fix what you've broken."

Teagan started to reply, but the phone went dead.

Sighing, Teagan paced back and forth, keeping her eyes on Cole. She had no choice but to go to the police station, and she'd have to take Cole with her. Hopefully, it wouldn't take too long, but she felt guilty about cutting his school trip short.

Teagan strolled over to Cole and gently pulled him away from his friends.

"Mom, did you see the photo booth with the dinosaur?"

"I see, honey. Cole, we have to leave early."

Cole's brows pinched together in a frown. "Why?"

"Something came up at work."

"But you promised. I can stay out of the way with my friends," Cole begged.

His disappointment sent a sting to her heart. "We won't be long, but we have dinner plans with the family, and we can reschedule a visit."

"What about lunch with my friends?"

"I just need an hour, tops."

"Promise?"

"Pinky promise." Teagan twined her pinky finger around Cole's.

Chapter Seven

Teagan spoke with Police Commissioner Ellis to find out where Penny Fernsby was being held as Jason navigated the traffic.

"Commissioner, it's my job to know when a high-profile foreign politician is taken into custody."

"That wasn't my call."

"Whose was it?" Teagan demanded.

"Police Captain Ethan at Seventh Precinct," Ellis informed her.

"Jason, take us to Seventh Precinct."

Making a quick turn at the light, Jason hit the gas, ignoring the angry honks from other drivers and shouts from people waiting to cross the street.

"Are we on a chase, Mom?" Cole asked excitedly.

"Sit back, Cole. I need you to listen to me and not interrupt."

"Okay."

"I'm going to the police station because something came up, but you may see some things you won't understand."

"Like what?"

"People yelling and cursing at me."

"Why?"

"I work for the president, and sometimes I have to do things that make other people angry."

"But you do those things to protect us, right?"

Teagan smiled at his innocent expression. "Exactly."

"Then people should be proud, like I am."

"You're proud of me, Cole?"

"Yeah, Mom. You're like Wonder Woman." Cole grinned and rested his head on her shoulder.

Teagan chuckled, wrapping an arm around him and kissing the top of his head. "Wonder Woman is way cooler than me."

Jason parked a few blocks from the precinct. Minister Fernsby being taken into custody had brought reporters from all over the country, hoping to get the big story.

"Stay with Jason," Teagan instructed Cole. "I'll be back soon."

Jason turned in his seat, looking over his shoulder. "Sure you'll be okay? There's a pretty big crowd."

"I'll be fine. Keep an eye on him."

Cole pressed his hand against the window as Teagan climbed out of the car. She pressed her hand against the glass over his and winked, blowing him a kiss as she turned away.

Teagan was fighting through the crowds to reach the police station when she was shoved in the shoulder by a woman holding a sign displaying Minister Fernsby and President Sanders' faces.

"Are you for the people?" the woman demanded, pointing the sign at Teagan's face.

"Back off," Teagan said, holding up her badge.

"Traitor! You're one of them!" the woman spat.

Ignoring the growing shouts, Teagan pushed inside and went straight to the front desk.

"Can I help you?" the officer on duty asked.

"I need to talk with Captain Ethan."

The officer flipped a pen idly in his hand. "And you are?"

Teagan narrowed her eyes. "The person who's going to decide if you receive a pension or not."

His mouth tightened as he picked up the phone. "Name?"

"Agent Teagan Stone on behalf of the President of the United States."

There was a commotion behind her, and she turned to see a few reporters pushing their way inside.

The officer dropped the phone and ran around the desk. "You can't be in here!"

"Why is the Minister of France being held here?" one of the reporters asked.

"Get back!" He shoved her.

"I have a right to be here." She pushed the microphone in his face as the cameraman filmed behind her.

Teagan took the opportunity to slip down the hallway, checking nameplates on doors until she found the captain's office.

Teagan pushed open his door. "Captain Ethan?"

"Who the hell are you?" Captain Ethan barked, holding a phone halfway to his ear. A young police officer stood beside his desk.

"The person who's going to save your ass."

The young officer's eyes widened. "I've seen you before."

"I don't give a damn who you are," Captain Ethan hissed.

The officer snapped his fingers. "Sir, this is Agent Stone. She works for President Sanders."

"Get out." Teagan and the Captain told him at the same time.

Captain Ethan frowned as the officer beat a hasty retreat. He stood and moved around his desk, getting in Teagan's face. "I suggest you leave with him."

"Get out of my face, Captain."

"Or what?"

The same officer stuck his head around the door. "Captain, we need you. There's a, uh, disturbance."

Teagan watched him leave and then went in search of the interrogation rooms.

"Minister Fernsby, you will be prosecuted as a terrorist!"

Teagan heard the raised voice as she passed a closed door. She shoved the door open, and two detectives reached for their guns.

"Don't say another word," Teagan told Minister Fernsby.

"We're questioning a suspect," the burlier of the two detectives snapped.

Teagan raised an eyebrow. "Without her lawyer present? I know she explained her credentials."

"Listen, if you're some bureaucrat from D.C., save it for someone who cares," he spat, moving toward her.

Teagan grabbed his wrist and yanked his arm behind his back.

"Ah! What the fuck are you doing?" the detective screamed.

"Teagan, we need to go," Minister Fernsby said.

A gunshot rang out.

"Cole!" Teagan released the detective and ran from the room.

Officers were shouting instructions to each other and drawing their weapons.

Teagan reached for her gun before remembering it was back in the car. "Shit!"

"Stay away from the windows," an officer cautioned.

"I need a gun."

"Ma'am, you're safer inside," he replied.

"My son is out there." Teagan's heart was pounding.

"We need to get the situation under control."

Teagan ignored him and ran from the building amid shouts and screams.

"Help!" an elderly woman cried out.

"Are you shot?" Teagan asked.

"Twisted my ankle trying to run," the woman explained.

"Stay low," Teagan said, checking her over.

Teagan looked up, scanning the high-rise buildings. "Where are you, you son of bitch?"

More gunshots rang out as Teagan sprinted back to the SUV. It was empty.

"Cole!" Teagan yelled, looking around in panic.

"Teagan!" Jason beckoned her from a side alley.

"Mommy!" Cole jumped into her arms as soon as she reached them.

"Are you hurt? Let me look at you." Teagan ran her hands over him to check he was in one piece before hugging him close.

"I heard the gunfire, and we hid behind the dumpster," Jason explained, nodding behind him.

"Thank you, Jason."

"Any leads?"

"No. I need to go back and get Minister Fernsby."

"Don't leave me, Mommy," Cole pleaded, clinging to her.

"Shush. You're safe, baby. I'm not going anywhere."

"I called Christian," Jason informed her.

"Thanks. I know he would've been worried."

"Oh, my god! She's been shot!"

Teagan pushed Cole behind her at the shriek. She ducked her head out the alley to see paramedics and Captain Ethan crowded around a body—Minister Fernsby.

"Oh, no," Teagan whispered. She left the alley and hurried toward the scene.

"Teagan!" Jason yelled.

"Mom!" Cole caught up with her, clutching her hand.

"Cole, wait here with Jason," Teagan said as Jason scooped him up.

Cole balled up his fists. "No. I want you, Mommy."

"She's coming right back, big guy," Jason reassured him.

Teagan ran to the EMTs as they continued to give Minister Fernsby CPR. "What happened?"

"Ma'am, we need you to stay back," the paramedic said as reporters and police flooded the area.

Teagan knew the news of this would only do more damage. "Get the cameras out of here!" she yelled at the police officers. She took a few deep breaths. Losing her cool would only escalate the situation. "Is she dead?" she asked the paramedic.

"Are you related?" the paramedic asked.

"Captain Ethan, we need to call the coroner," the paramedic said grimly.

"Wait." Teagan's hands shook as she approached the stretcher.

"Fatal shot to the chest," the paramedic explained, pulling the sheet over Penny Fernsby's body.

"I...I need to call the president," Teagan said, her voice choked with emotion.

"I'm sorry," Captain Ethan said awkwardly.

His apology was empty. Teagan was furious. This could have been avoided. He'd had Penny Fernsby brought in for questioning so he could look like some big shot.

Before she could think, Teagan punched him straight in the nose as the cameras captured everything.

"Oh, my god!" a woman in the crowd screamed.

Teagan wriggled her hand, shaking off the pain. "Shut the fuck up."

Chapter Eight

A *Few Days Later* Jeff basked in the outcome of his work. After putting a bullet in Wilde's girlfriend, he'd returned home to watch the news coverage. Leaving the building across from the police station had been as simple as changing into one of the security teams' clothes left hanging in the office staff room. He'd collected his car a few blocks from the crime scene and drove away just as they blocked off the streets.

He hadn't planned to kill Fernsby, but he'd wanted to put as much fear and uncertainty into the city as possible.

Sitting back in his lounge chair, he chuckled as they replayed Minister of Defense Penny Fernsby's funeral, with US and French politicians showing their love and respect for the long-standing government official.

"President Sanders is now giving a speech," a GNS reporter announced.

"*To the American people and our friends and allies in France , I want to send our deepest condolences. The events that transpired in New York were a travesty, and we will use every resource available to find the person or people responsible. Minister Fernsby was a longtime friend, and I will personally oversee the investigation into her murder."*

"Earlier today, President Sanders sent a message to Prime Minister Perly of France," the GNS reporter continued, and the footage switched to President Sanders and Prime Minister Perly shaking hands at the White House. Footage of Congressman Wilde's body being wheeled out of the Arlo Hotel flashed on the screen, followed by Minister Fernsby's body being removed from Seventh Precinct.

Sitting back in his chair, Jeff tossed popcorn into his mouth as the reporters explained how the killings had all occurred in the city, and people were terrified. His thoughts turned briefly to Claire. The only thing he missed about her was her cooking. Constantly eating out was expensive, and he needed to save money. Over the past few days, he'd considered looking for a new job or selling his home.

The doorbell rang, and Jeff checked the camera on his phone to see his mother-in-law on the porch. Claire's mother hadn't been by their house for months after he'd complained that she was interfering in their business too much. Claire complained to her mother about him, which had always led to a fight.

He stood and turned off the TV, marching upstairs and locking the basement door. He opened the front door with a grim expression. "Peggy, what are you doing here?"

"Is Claire here?"

"No."

"I haven't talked to her in a few weeks. I tried calling, but she never picks up."

Jeff shrugged. "She told me she was going on a girl's trip."

"When?" Peggy looked over his shoulder, seeing the newspapers strewn on the couch, dirty clothes on the floor, and takeout boxes scattered around.

"About a week ago."

Her mouth tightened. "Have you talked to her?"

"Briefly, but she made me promise I wouldn't call and disturb her girl's trip." Jeff shrugged again.

Peggy had never liked Jeff. No, that wasn't true—she despised him but had kept her mouth shut over the years. Claire was her only child, and she hadn't wanted to alienate her when she'd come home full of unrealistic dreams Jeff had implanted in her mind. The minute Claire had said they were getting married, she'd known her daughter would always be under his spell. Yes, he was good-looking, but he didn't come from a wealthy background that could support her baby girl like she deserved. Claire getting hurt at her job and no longer able to work had ended her career dreams.

"I can't believe she wouldn't call me," Peggy said, stepping up to the front door to go inside.

Jeff blocked her from entering.

"Can I come in?"

"I'm busy."

She arched an eyebrow. "Busy with what?"

"Work."

"It will only take a minute. Maybe I can call Claire from your phone."

Jeff forced a smile and stepped aside, realizing she wouldn't take no for an answer.

Peggy wrinkled her nose at the trash in the living room. "When was the last time you cleaned up?"

Jeff locked the door behind him, facing Peggy as she sat on the couch. "Right before Claire left."

"Claire told me you never help with the upkeep around here, Jeff," Peggy accused.

Jeff's gaze flicked around the room. He plucked a cushion from the couch as Peggy continued to yap on about Claire not checking in with her.

"Jeff, do you hear me?" Peggy demanded. "I asked if I could use your phone."

"I hear you, Peggy." Jeff moved quickly, smashing the cushion into her face.

"What are you—" Peggy screamed and fought to push him away as he leaned his weight on her, ramming the cushion over her mouth and nose for endless minutes until her thrashing stopped.

"Bitch." Jeff mumbled as he stood and looked down at his dead mother-in-law. The high from killing was becoming addictive.

"You can join your daughter on her girl's trip now." Jeff chuckled as he returned to the basement for a large plastic bag to dispose of her body once night fell.

* * *

Teagan listened intently as President Sanders and Prime Minister Perly shouted back and forth in a closed-door meeting.

She'd received an urgent summons to get to D.C. for a briefing. The press was eating Sanders alive by spewing his weakness as a leader and letting Beau Perly dictate what the US should be doing to capture the killer.

Being back in D.C. came at the cost of Teagan missing an appointment with Dr. Falk. Christian had argued against her leaving so soon after Cole's traumatic experience and had demanded they schedule time for him to talk with the doctor. Sean had been gone for almost a year, and witnessing the shootout had brought out a different side of Christian. Remembering his angry shouting brought tears to her eyes.

"My son was almost killed!" Christian poked a finger at her.

Teagan's mouth quivered as tears pooled in her eyes. He was distraught and felt helpless at being unable to help and comfort his wife and child, and he blamed Teagan.

"This job is going to kill you and our family."

Teagan wiped the tears on her cheeks. "Christian, listen to me."

"No! Our son is in our bedroom right now, terrified to sleep after what happened." The veins in his forehead stood out.

Christian's words were painful. He hadn't stooped to that level since they'd had a terrible fight a few years back when she wasn't spending enough time with him. To him, marriage meant forever, and she'd slacked off. For her job to affect his kids' safety after Broderick and Stanton kidnapping him and the kids for leverage still pissed him off.

"Agent Stone, are you listening?" President Sanders challenged, bringing Teagan back to the present.

"I can't stay," she whispered.

"What?" Both men asked as she stood.

"Sir, I apologize for leaving so abruptly, but I want to assure you that we will catch the man who killed Minister Fernsby."

"You are the director of the agency, correct?" Prime Minister Perly asked, his eyes narrowing on Teagan.

"I am, and as such, you need to step away and let me do my job. Perhaps then, you'll get some clarity on what's happening right in front of you."

"Who is she?" Prime Minister Perly demanded, looking at President Sanders. "I'm not taking bullshit from the likes of her."

"Her methods may not be conventional, but she's the best, Beau," President Sanders defended Teagan.

"Returning to my country without the person or people responsible for Minister Fernsby's murder is unacceptable."

President Sanders sighed heavily. "I understand how you feel, but we can't lock someone up for the sake of it just to appease the public outcry."

"Then I suggest you find a way to prepare your country for what's coming."

"What is that supposed to mean?" President Sanders narrowed his eyes at the French leader.

Prime Minister Perly stood and buttoned his jacket. "You may have gotten your way with the previous prime minister, but I'm not him."

Prime Minister Beau Perly turned and left the room without waiting for a reply.

"What are the chances this case will get solved in time?" President Sanders asked wearily.

Teagan sat in her seat and ran a hand over her face. "World War Three will never be an option, Mr. President."

"I hope you're right, Agent Stone. Find whoever's behind this."

"Yes, Sir."

President Sanders stood to leave but then paused at the door. "And Teagan?"

"Yes, Sir?"

"Take care of yourself."

Chapter Nine

Dr. Falk waited for Teagan to speak as she stared out her office window. Christian wanted them to have family counseling, but Dr. Falk felt it best to talk with Teagan alone before including Cole. Usually, her fights with Christian were resolved quickly, but it had been two days since they'd spoken.

Teagan cleared her throat.

"Take your time," Dr. Falk encouraged.

"I messed up."

"What do you mean?"

"Taking my son with me to the police station."

"You didn't know something like that would happen, Teagan."

"My job is to know and anticipate everything."

"Are you a psychic?" Dr. Falk joked.

Teagan chuckled. It was the first time she'd laughed for days. "No."

"Then removing that burden is best for your mental health and your family's."

"When I saw how scared Cole was, I couldn't help

thinking, what if one of those bullets..." Teagan trailed off, her throat clogged with tears.

Dr. Falk handed her the box of tissues. Teagan took one and dabbed her eyes. "We've discussed how important your role is at the agency."

"I never wanted to go back into the firm."

"But?"

"Something in me felt like it was unfinished. I see the bad in the world and want to do my part to balance things, even if only a little."

"Do you feel you're doing that at the expense of your family?"

Teagan nodded. "My son could have died."

"I talked with Cole. He doesn't blame you."

"Christian blames me. I see it in his eyes."

"He's upset at the situation, not at you."

"He won't talk to me."

"Are you trying to talk to him?" Dr. Falk challenged.

Teagan thought about the question. She knew she was being just as petty by ignoring him when they were in bed together. Usually, they cuddled and talked about their day, but she'd been avoiding him too.

"It seems to me that you're punishing yourself."

"What do you mean?"

"You're carrying the guilt on your shoulders whenever something happens that you can't control. I see in your eyes, Teagan."

"Being a mom, a wife, and having a career means I have to carry the load."

Dr. Falk linked her hands in her lap. "Carrying the load doesn't mean allowing it to bury you. It's okay to ask for help."

"All I can think is, what if Jason hadn't been there? I told Cole to stay in the car."

"You made a mistake."

"I'm trying to release some of the workload before I burn out."

"Good. You're the boss, but you can't handle everything. Besides, if people are slacking around you, perhaps it's time to see if they'd be better utilized elsewhere."

"You mean fire them?" Teagan's mouth twitched, but then she frowned as an idea came to her.

"What is it?" Dr. Falk asked, seeing Teagan's expression.

"Fire them," Teagan repeated.

"Huh?"

Teagan stood. "You said fire them."

"I didn't put it like that. I mean, you have to consider their job performance—"

Teagan snapped her fingers. "Yes! History of their job performance." She grabbed her purse and phone. "I need to go."

"Wait." Dr. Falk jumped up. "Your husband and son are outside."

Teagan slapped her forehead. "You're right."

Dr. Falk glanced at the clock on the wall. "Can whatever you're rushing off for wait for another hour?"

Teagan nodded. "I need to send a quick text," she said, removing her phone from her purse as Dr. Falk went to the door and told Christian to come inside with Cole.

Teagan: *Check the background of Congressmen Wilde's staff.*

Spider: *We've already narrowed it down to three people.*

Teagan: *Any disgruntled employees?*

Christian and Cole stepped into the room, and Teagan hugged her son.

"Thanks for waiting, Christian and Cole. Teagan has made some great progress," Dr. Falk informed them.

Teagan's phone dinged, and she looked down to see Spider's response.

Spider: *Two.*

"Are you working right now?" Christian fussed, sitting across from her.

"Christian, I think she's made a break in the case. Usually, I would agree to leave work out of our session, but this is a sensitive situation," Dr. Falk explained.

Teagan put her phone back in her purse. "Cole, Mommy is sorry for putting you in a situation that could have put you in danger." Teagan stretched her arms out for a hug.

He smiled and jumped into them. "I forgive you, Mommy. It's not your fault."

"Thank you, baby." Teagan kissed his cheek.

"Can you and Daddy make up now?" Cole asked, grabbing her and Christian's hands and bringing them together.

"Cole, it doesn't work like that," Christian replied.

"But you said to always apologize when you hurt someone's feelings," he argued.

"Cole is right, Christian," Dr. Falk agreed.

"Christian, I can't apologize enough. I haven't stopped beating myself up about what could have happened to Cole," Teagan said softly.

Christian ran a hand over his face. "I know you are, Teagan." He squeezed her hand.

"Cole, do you mind stepping out of the room for a second?" Dr. Falk asked.

Cole nodded and kissed Teagan's cheek before leaving the room.

"Speak freely," Dr. Falk said to Teagan and Christian.

"My son almost died. I want Teagan to understand she's not Wonder Woman and that it cannot happen again," Christian said.

"You're right." Teagan agreed, running a hand up his arm.

"You should have left him safe with the teachers and his friends or called me to pick him up."

Dr. Falk frowned. "Is there a part of you that blames yourself, Christian?" Dr. Falk asked.

Teagan cupped his face. "Baby, it wasn't your fault. I take full blame. I'll never let us get to this place again."

"Us avoiding each other around the kids," Christian teased, interlocking their hands.

Teagan smiled. "We were both wrong on that front."

"Remember, you're both human, which comes with all kinds of feelings. But communicating and listening to each other is so important," Dr. Falk advised.

"Dr. Falk, thanks for seeing us on short notice," Christian said, kissing Teagan's knuckles.

"Thank you, Dr. Falk." Teagan extended her hand for a shake.

Dr. Falk smiled as she walked them to the door. "That's what I'm here for. Call me if you need to talk again."

Christian and Teagan grasped Cole's hand as they left Dr. Falk's office and headed for their car. Christian held the door for her, and Cole got in the backseat.

"Can we have tacos for dinner?" Cole poked his head between the seats as Christian started the car.

"We have everything at home to make tacos, so I don't

see why not," Christian said, reversing out of the parking space.

"Tacos night sounds great to me." Teagan high-fived Cole.

"Yes!" Cole sat back in his seat.

Teagan smiled at Christian as he turned into traffic.

"Dr. Falk said you made a breakthrough with the case?" Christian questioned when they stopped at a light.

"Hopefully, if my guess is right."

"Do you need to leave?"

Deep down, Teagan wanted to be there with her team to make the arrest, but being with her family was more important. Calling President Sanders and giving him an update could be done from home.

"No. Spider is handling it."

"So we have you all to ourselves," Christian teased, caressing her cheek.

"Gross," Cole muttered, and his parents laughed.

The light turned green, and Christian drove home feeling like he'd won the lottery.

Chapter Ten

Spider strummed his fingers on his thigh. He closed his eyes and mouthed a few words of prayer for himself and the team.

They'd obtained a list of Congressman Wilde's ex-employees who had conflicts with him. At first, his secretary had tried to derail them from investigating his office, but when Gregory showed her the evidence of her stealing from the campaign funds, she backed off and let them work.

Spider was speechless that Koen Wilde had lasted so long in politics with the number of enemies he'd made. The team had discovered that Koen had paid off high-profile lobbyists to get in the same rooms as senators and members of Congress. He'd lined the lobbyists' pockets with blood money to reach the top. Koen's underhanded methods would have been discovered eventually, but he'd been murdered before he could be brought up on charges.

Daughtrey found the first name on the list—Jacob Rowley, married with three children and laid off two years ago. Broderick checked his gun while Gregory pulled on his bulletproof vest. It was early evening when they rolled up in a quiet neighborhood.

Teagan usually led them on missions, but she was spending time with her family. Spider understood after hearing what had happened with Cole. Teagan and Christian's kids were like his nieces and nephews. He'd give his life for them at the drop of a dime.

Spider glanced at his team in the back of the black van. "Daughtrey and Gregory, I want you two in the back. He may try to run."

Both men nodded and hopped out of the van.

"I'm ready." Broderick pushed the door open.

Spider followed with his badge on display and the warrant in his hand. As they stepped into Jacob Rowley's yard, the door opened to reveal a bald, middle-aged man with a large belly and a baby boy on his hip. A young girl peered out from behind his legs.

"Can I help you?" he asked.

"Jacob Rowley?" Spider started up the steps, keeping eye contact with the man.

"Yeah. Who are you?"

"We'd like to ask you some questions downtown."

"Questions about what?"

"Sir, are you home alone?"

"My kids are here. What's this about?"

"You worked for Congressman Koen Wilde, correct?"

Looking from Broderick to Spider, Jacob wrapped a hand around his daughter's hand and nodded.

"Can we come in and look around?"

"Is this about those shootings?"

"Mr. Rowley, it would be best if we did this inside," Spider suggested.

"I didn't kill him. I'm glad he's dead, but it wasn't me," Jacob stated.

Broderick cocked his head. "Do you really want your kids to hear our conversation?"

"I have nothing to hide. Koen was a dick."

Jacob stepped back to allow them entry, and Spider motioned for Broderick to search the small brick house. Scanning the living room, he noticed toys lying around and the TV playing Disney programs.

Jacob put his baby son down in the playpen and told his daughter to go play in her room. "Ask anybody who worked for Wilde, and they'll all tell you the same," he said, sagging into his chair.

"Where were you on the night of his shooting?"

"Working," Jacob answered.

"Where do you work?"

"I'm a security guard for a construction company."

Spider removed his notepad from his pocket. "How long have you been employed there?"

"About two years now. Since I got fired. My brother-in-law got me the job." Jacob reached for a blanket to cover his son.

"We're going to need your employer's name and your wife's phone number."

"Nothing back there," Broderick said as he came back down the hall.

Jacob glared. "Happy now?"

"We have a warrant to bring you in for questioning, but seeing as you have two kids and you've cooperated fully, I'm giving you a pass," Spider told him.

Jacob gestured between Broderick and Spider. "Don't you work for some big agency? I've seen you on TV."

Spider and Broderick were saved from answering as

the door opened, and a woman entered carrying grocery bags.

"Jacob, why are the cops outside—" She stopped as she saw Spider and Broderick.

Jacob jumped out of his seat to help her with the bags. "Babe, they're here about those shootings on the news."

Trudy placed her purse and coat in the closet and walked over to check on her son. "Jacob wouldn't hurt a fly."

"Will decide that, ma'am," Spider said, observing their interaction with each other.

"If you have any other questions, my husband and I would prefer you speak with our lawyer." Trudy opened the front door for us to leave.

"We'll be in touch if we have more questions. Don't leave town," Spider advised.

Trudy and Jacob stood at the front door, watching as Broderick and Spider returned to their vehicle.

"We'll keep a cop car on them tonight while Gregory looks into their alibi," Spider said, climbing into the van.

Checking off Jacob's name, Spider typed in Jeff Shepherd. A former employee of Koen Wilde got fired because a misconduct report was filed on Koen for being inappropriate in the workplace, and Jeff covered for him. When the time came to pay Jeff back for taking the fall, Wilde fired him months later. The scandal rocked the offices of the D.C. halls, but no one went to bat for Jeff. The woman who filed the complaint transferred to another state and blocked all calls and notifications from Jeff when he needed support to get his name cleared.

Spider grasped his phone to call Teagan and give her an update.

"Hey, did you see this?" Gregory asked.

All heads turned to him.

"What?" Spider asked.

"He's a trained sniper," Gregory said.

"Shit." Daughtrey hit the gas harder.

"Why are we just now hearing about Jeff Shepherd?" Spider snatched the computer from Gregory.

"You know as well as me we've been dealing with non-stop crap trying to get through red tape," Gregory challenged.

"No excuses. I need to let Teagan know. How much longer, Daughtrey?" Spider barked.

"About another twenty minutes," Daughtrey responded.

"Hello?" Teagan answered the phone. "Tatum, sit down and eat your food."

"It's me," Spider said.

"Any leads?"

"Maybe, and it's a big one."

"What do you mean?"

"Jeff Shepherd is a former employee of Wilde's. And he's a trained sniper."

Teagan gasped. "You're kidding?"

"Nope. I guess we need to have another conversation with the president. We could have avoided wasting time if the proper channels were working," Spider said.

"What about Jacob Rowley?"

"He seemed harmless. Scared of his own shadow."

"Do what you need to do to catch him," Teagan instructed.

"We're heading to the address now."

"Send the information. I'll call the police captain in that district for cover."

"All taken care of. Focus on your family."

"Are you sure?"

"Positive. We can handle him, Boss."

"Be safe," Teagan said.

"Thanks, Boss." Spider chuckled when he heard the kids in the background yelling at each other over the remote.

Twenty minutes later, Daughtrey parked a few houses down from Jeff's door and turned off the engine. The neighborhood seemed to be family-friendly. At almost eight at night, kids played in the yard while elderly couples sat out on their porches.

"No car. He may not be home," Daughtrey observed.

Gazing around the area, Spider noticed a few abandoned apartments up the block. "I want the block shut down at both ends." He leaned forward, looking through his binoculars.

"Undercover is here in unmarked cars," Daughtrey said.

"Let's wait a few more minutes to see if more people go inside first," Spider suggested.

Broderick grunted. "If he's home, he probably knows we're here."

"I'm more worried about civilians getting hurt." Spider watched some kids run into their house.

"Check this out." Daughtrey tapped Spider on the shoulder.

Spider followed his eye line to Jeff's door and saw him carrying out the trash. He waved at an older woman on her porch and walked back into his house.

"Likes to pretend he's a good guy," Daughtrey observed.

"Come on. We need to end this now." Spider dropped the binoculars on the seat and shut the van door.

His team followed, and Gregory approached the older woman on her front porch, showing her his badge. "Ma'am, we need you to come with us for your safety."

"Why? What's going on?" Gregory helped the woman as she struggled to get up. "A police situation, ma'am," he said, escorting her to a neighbor's house down the street.

Spider knocked on Jeff's door and waited. When there was no reply, he banged his fist on the surface. A few seconds passed before the door slowly opened. No one was there.

Reaching for his gun, Spider cocked his head, listening for movement. "Jeff Shepherd! This is the FBI. Come out with your hands up."

Broderick and Spider shared a glance as they waited for a response. Slowly stepping inside, they took in the dirty clothes, flies, and stench in the air from the rotting food. Coughing, they covered their noses as best as they could.

"He's the guy," Daughtrey muttered.

"Fuck you!"

Bullets sprayed from nowhere. Spider and Broderick ducked as Daughtrey moved behind the wall. Leaning forward, Daughtrey saw Spider behind the second wall near the kitchen, and they made eye contact. Daughtrey laid down covering fire, allowing Spider to edge closer to the door in the corner, which he presumed led to the basement.

"Give it up, Jeff!" Spider yelled.

More gunfire met his request.

Spider kicked the door open and angled his gun at Jeff. "Don't move."

Broderick covered Spider, his gun also aimed at Jeff.

Spider eased down the stairs and kicked the gun away from Jeff, pushing him onto his stomach. "Anybody else in the house?"

"I want my lawyer."

"Are you confessing?" Spider and Broderick lifted him off the floor to sit in the chair.

Jeff grinned. "Nothing to confess."

Chapter Eleven

"What is he saying?" Teagan marched into the briefing room and removed her jacket. She glanced at the live feed of Jeff handcuffed to the table. Daughtrey and Broderick stood on either side of him.

"Nothing right now," Spider replied.

"Any casualties?"

"No. A bullet grazed his arm, but he'll live."

"He's a former sniper?"

"Yeah. Koen hired him because they knew each other from the Army," Spider explained.

"Hired and fired by the guy who knew all his secrets," Teagan murmured.

"What are you thinking?"

"He's talked to you and said nothing. I could try. See where his head is."

"And if the usual tactics don't work?" Spider implored.

"The firm directs me to use all available methods to

secure a confession." Teagan left the room, rolling up her sleeves.

Teagan knocked on the door of the interrogation room. Daughtrey checked the peephole and unlocked the door to allow her to enter.

"Have you given him water?" Teagan questioned.

"He refuses," Broderick growled.

Teagan turned to Jeff. "Mr. Shepherd, we want you to be comfortable."

"Why? So you can torture me longer?" Jeff grunted.

Teagan smirked. "Yes."

Sitting across from him, she motioned for Broderick and Daughtrey to leave them alone.

Daughtrey frowned. "Are you sure?"

"Mr. Shepherd is chained to the table. He's not going anywhere. We can have a civilized conversation. Right, Jeff? Can I call you Jeff?" Teagan crossed her legs and interlocked her hands.

"I want my lawyer."

"So, you're a sniper," Teagan said, ignoring his request.

Jeff's eyes narrowed into slits. "And? What do you know about serving your country?"

Teagan leaned back in her chair. "I read your file. Forty-seven years old, wife, no children, and worked for Koen Wilde for seven years until he fired you."

Jeff ignored her statement.

"We're running your prints as we speak. It would be in your interests to confess."

Jeff pressed his lips together.

"Do you think you're leaving here, Jeff? I promise you that's not happening."

Lowering his head, Jeff cracked his neck. "He deserved what happened to him."

"Why?"

"Because he's just like the rest of them. Out for himself."

"What about the other three killings?"

"I did them a favor."

Teagan folded her arms over her chest. "We've tried to get in contact with your wife. Is she dead?"

"She's dead."

Teagan looked at the one-way mirror, knowing Spider would already be arranging the team to look into his wife's disappearance.

"Did you kill your wife, Jeff?"

He grinned. "I want my lawyer."

"Don't play games with me, Jeff. My son was there the day you killed Minister Fernsby."

Jeff shrugged. "Kids will learn that's life."

"You see that mirror, Jeff? No one cares if I kill you, so whatever happens in this room, I'll go home to my family. Unlike you."

Jeff growled and lunged at Teagan, only to be yanked back by the handcuffs. "Fuck you and everyone else who was killed!"

"You were sloppy. The skills you believe you have won't work in your favor."

"He deserved to die!"

"I asked you the whereabouts of your wife, Mr. Shepherd. Confess, and maybe we can negotiate the death penalty."

"We all have to live with our choices."

Broderick reentered the room and bent to whisper in her ear, "We found his mother-in-law's body a few blocks away from his house. We got prints. He didn't clean up too well."

"Search for his wife."

Jeff chuckled at her words. "I shipped her off."

Teagan looked at him. "What did you say?"

"My wife is on a trip."

"Where?"

"At sea." Jeff's laugh was maniacal.

"At sea, huh? Something tells me you're hurt. I can see the pain in your eyes. You've been bamboozled by Koen and probably had marriage issues because your wife wanted to leave you after you lost your job. Maybe Koen had it right from the start."

"That's bullshit! I put years of my life into that job. Wilde owed me," Jeff seethed through his teeth.

"He owed you? You thought you were special? Koen was a corrupt, vile piece of shit, and you were his puppet. You let him get away with hurting people."

"Fuck you, bitch!"

"We have your mother-in-law's body, and your prints are all over the gun in the basement. Did you think we wouldn't find your bag with the map and location of each shooting?"

Jeff jerked his hands against the handcuffs. "I want my lawyer."

"Too late. You'd better pray I don't execute you right here, motherfucker."

"I want my lawyer, bitch!" Jeff screamed over and over.

Leaving the interrogation room, Teagan told Broderick and Daughtrey to lock him up until he could be shipped to federal prison.

* * *

The press secretary stood at the podium in the briefing room, taking questions as they waited for President Sanders. Behind him was the team from D.C. to inform the public about the killer.

"The press is waiting outside once we're done in here," Spider murmured beside her.

Teagan nodded. "The cameras haven't left since we moved in on him."

"I'd like to introduce President Sanders," the press secretary announced to the briefing room.

"Mr. President, what do you think of the suspect being an ex-employee?" a reporter shouted across the room.

President Sanders faced the audience, reading over his statement. "Like many other Americans, I am grateful to our law enforcement, FBI, and The Firm for taking the necessary steps to capture the murderer."

"Are you afraid a copycat is out there?"

President Sanders held up his hands to pause the shouting. "Before I answer questions, I want to let the public know we will continue to monitor and work with the local police for everyone's safety. Director Stone?" President Sanders nodded to Teagan, who moved to stand behind the podium.

"Forgive me. I'm not usually in front of the camera." Teagan cleared her throat. "As the case is ongoing, we can't reveal specific information. My team and I have taken Jeff Shepherd into custody. Mr. Shepherd is a former government employee and trained sniper responsible for the murders in New York."

"Is it true Prime Minister Perly is contemplating the

French relationship with the US?" a reporter from GNS news asked.

"I won't be discussing foreign affairs," Teagan said firmly. "Any other questions?"

"Are we to believe it was one man working alone?" the reporter continued to probe.

"Yes, we are confident it was one person working alone," Teagan confirmed.

The press secretary interrupted and took the microphone. "We will give you all a detailed list of the information we've discussed and move all questions to the US office."

Teagan, President Sanders, and the team thanked the reporters and left the briefing room.

President Sanders entered his office, keeping the door open for Teagan to follow. "I know you're ready to get back to your family."

"I am, sir."

President Sanders took a seat at his desk. "Prime Minister Perly sends his thanks. Even though we disagreed on the process, we're back to being partners."

"Glad to hear that, Mr. President."

"How is Jeff Shepherd being treated?"

"It was filed under terroristic threats."

President Sanders signed off on some documents as he talked, and the secretary appeared with a glass of water. "I want him on lockdown twenty-four-seven. He can't get off on a technicality."

"No, sir. He confessed."

"Thank you. When are you going on vacation?" President Sanders asked as Teagan turned to leave.

"As soon as my boss gives me some time off," she chuckled, leaving him in laughter.

Chapter Twelve

A Month Later—New York

Teagan concluded her meeting with Celine, handing off all the latest reports to file while she was away. She'd pushed back all her appointments, and President Sanders had finally cleared her to take time off. Spider would handle things in the office while she was on vacation with her family.

Jeff Shepherd was still locked up and pleading insanity. President Sanders was working with the local officials to ensure he went to trial as soon as possible.

Spider knocked on her door as she grabbed her purse and briefcase. "Heading out?"

"Yep, so whatever it is, you can handle it."

"The boys wanted to know if you're coming back," Spider teased, picking up the stack of files she'd left for him and following her from the office.

"I'll be back. It's only two weeks."

They walked down the hall, and Spider pressed the elevator button for the parking garage. "Jason going with you?"

"Yeah." Teagan rolled her eyes. "President Sanders wants me to keep my detail while I'm gone."

"He's right. The copycat killer saw your face that day at the press conference."

"That was too much. I'd rather stay in the background."

They stepped onto the elevator, and Teagan pulled out her phone to call Christian.

"What are you guys doing?" she asked as she heard her kids playing in the background.

"On our way to pick you up," Christian explained.

"You don't have to do that. Jason will come scoop you up."

"I called Jason to come grab us, and we loaded up the car. We're driving directly to the airport."

"I still need to take care of a few things before we leave."

"Teagan, this vacation is happening. Spider can handle the office," Christian stated.

The elevator doors opened to reveal her husband standing next to the Escalade with the phone to his ear. He was wearing a huge grin. All the kids were with him, holding flowers to greet her. Teagan ended the call with her mouth agape.

"Did you know he was here?" she asked Spider.

"Yeah. I was supposed to distract you," he admitted.

Teagan hugged her kids and then her husband, feeling like her old self again.

"Mommy, are you ready for our trip?" Tatum reached her arms around her waist.

"I am, Tatum. You look so pretty, baby."

"Grammy did my hair." She giggled, and Teagan pressed a kiss to her cheek.

Teagan looked at her husband. "Christian?"

"Yeah?" He took her purse and briefcase from her hands and tossed them in the back of the vehicle.

"Surprises are not my thing."

"Tell that to the President of the United States." Christian kissed her, and they climbed into the car. They held hands as they drove out of the garage.

* * *

Jamaica's beauty captured Teagan's heart. She relaxed on the beach as the kids played in the water with the nanny. Christian sat across from her in the hammock, immersed in his magazine while she read We Lie Here, the latest release from her favorite author, Rachel Howzell Hall. She sipped her pink virgin mojito, watching her kids have fun.

"I love it out here." Teagan placed her drink back on the table.

"Me, too. We can do this every year, maybe just the two of us next time."

"An anniversary trip." Teagan smiled.

Moving to his side, he stared at her. "Dr. Falk was right that we needed to stay on top of the two of us being in sync. I love you, Teagan."

"I love—"

Before she could reply, her cell phone rang. Teagan wanted to ignore it and spend quality time with her husband, but it was an unlisted number, which could only be one person.

Christian waited for her to decide. Teagan sighed and grabbed the phone. Just as Christian turned to face the water, she declined the call, turned off the phone, and put it away in her bag.

"Are you sure?"

"Positive. Spider can handle it. Come on. Let's go in the water." Teagan rose from the hammock, stretching her hand out for him to take. Christian surprised her by hoisting her into his arms, and she laughed as he ran into the water.

Standing off on the side and watching the family closely, Jason took the call. "Yes, Mr. President, she's here. I'll tell her."

He was torn about interrupting the family moment, but his job called for him to be the eyes and ears for Agent Stone at all times.

* * *

I hope you enjoyed Teagan's story so far. Please also check out **"Agent Red (Pursuit) Teagan Stone Book 8" sneak peek** with a host of intertwined characters.

Also, if you love Mystery, Suspense check out **"Mirror of Lies Book 1"** https://books2read.com/u/mgjEPx

Another thriller, crime fiction **"Ruined Book 1"** https://books2read.com/u/bzVGAj

Check out a free short here: ***"The Firm"*** https://payhip.com/b/py7S

Grab Boxset **"Agent Red 1-3"** here https://payhip.com/b/1KcxY

Sneak Peek Agent Red Fatal Pursuit Book 8

A fast-paced action adventure and political thriller with unforgettable characters and heart-pounding suspense.

Teagan Stone is on foreign ground, once again trying to defend the country she has vowed to protect. US military weapons have been stolen, and Teagan has gone undercover to unravel a conspiracy before the weapons are used against them. In a race against time, Teagan identifies suspects but soon learns that danger lies much closer to home.

Will Teagan unravel the plot against her country before their enemies prevail and war ensues?

Reading Order of Mirror Series

Mirror of Lies Book 1
> https://books2read.com/u/mgjEPx
> Mirror of Lust Book 2
> https://books2read.com/u/mVRpz2
> Mirror of Danger Book 3
> Mirror of Murder Book 4

Teagan Stone Reading Order of Series

1.Agent Red—Fatal Memory Book 1
https://books2read.com/u/4j2PYX
2.Agent Red—Fatal Target Book 2
https://books2read.com/u/bWP8Jq
3.Agent Red—Fatal Crime Book 3
https://books2read.com/u/mZadZJ
4.Agent Red—Fatal Justice Book 4
https://books2read.com/u/mqo7wd
5.Agent Red—Fatal Enemy Book 5
https://books2read.com/u/bxeo1q
6. Agent Red—Fatal Death Book 6
https://books2read.com/u/mqwlRv
7. Agent Red—Fatal Revenge Book 7
https://books2read.com/u/3JnKyA
8. Agent Red—Fatal Pursuit Book 8
https://books2read.com/u/bOPowo
9. Agent Red—Fatal Attack Book 9
10. Agent Red—Fatal Mission Book 10

What's Next?

Want to know what happens next? Follow me at the links below to catch the next release.

Thank you so much for reading, and if you enjoyed the crazy ride and decided to leave a review, we'd truly appreciate the support. Reviews are the lifeblood of the publishing world. They're read, appreciated, and needed. Please consider taking the time to leave a few words on Goodreads or BookBub.

Sign up for updates and sneak peeks at the sites below:

www.authoravasking.com
www.bookbub.com/avasking
www.goodreads.com/author/avasking
www.Twitter.com/authoravaking
www.Instagram.com/authoravasking
www.Facebook.com/authoravasking
www.304publishing.tumblr.com

Acknowledgments

I want to thank my team, who helps me behind the scenes, from my editors to my test readers and graphic designers, and the list goes on. I truly appreciate each of you for keeping me on my toes.

About the Author

Ava S. King is the debut author of thriller, mystery, suspense, and psychological crime novels.

If you want to know when the next book will come out, please visit Author Ava S. King website at http://www.authoravasking.com, where you can sign up to receive an email for her next release.

About 304 Publishing Company

We showcase authors writing romance, women's fiction, horror, erotica, crime fiction, fantasy, paranormal, sifi, thrillers, suspense novels, poetry collections, and beauty & style books.

Join our mailing list to stay updated with new releases and blog posts.

www.ingramcontent.com/pod-product-compliance
Lightning Source LLC
Chambersburg PA
CBHW011225190726
48287CB00008B/2752